UNICORN RIDERS

We Ride As One

To my children and all those who believe in unicorns — AD
To my children, Clare and Max — JB

Picture Window Books are published by Capstone,
1710 Roe Crest Drive, North Mankato, Minnesota 56003
www.mycapstone.com

Text © 2017 Aleesah Darlison
Illustrations © 2017 Jill Brailsford

Library of Congress Cataloging-in-Publication Data
Names: Darlison, Aleesah, author. | Brailsford, Jill, illustrator.
Title: Willow's victory / by Aleesah Darlison; illustrated by Jill Brailsford.
Description: North Mankato, Minnesota : Picture Window Books, [2017] |
   Series: Unicorn riders | Summary: The Unicorn Riders are attending the
   Spring Tournament, but in addition to the pressure of competition they have
   been warned that someone may be trying to sabotage the contest, and it is up
   to them to prevent that from happening.
Identifiers: LCCN 2016037800| ISBN 9781479565498 (library binding) |
   ISBN 9781479565573 (paperback)
Subjects: LCSH: Unicorns—Juvenile fiction. | Magic—Juvenile fiction. |
   Sports tournaments—Juvenile fiction. | Sabotage—Juvenile fiction. |
   Adventure stories. | CYAC: Unicorns—Fiction. | Magic—Fiction. |
   Contests—Fiction. | Sabotage—Fiction. | Adventure and adventurers—
   Fiction. | GSAFD: Adventure fiction. | LCGFT: Action and adventure fiction.
Classification: LCC PZ7.1.D333 Wm 2017 | DDC 813.6 [Fic] —dc23
LC record available at https://lccn.loc.gov/2016037800

Editor: Nikki Potts
Designer: Kayla Rossow
Art Director: Juliette Peters
Production Specialist: Kathy McColley
The illustrations in this book were created by Jill Brailsford.

Cover design by Walker Books Australia Pty Ltd
Cover images: Rider, symbol, and unicorns © Gillian Brailsford 2011;
lined paper © iStockphoto.com/Imageegaml;
parchment © iStockphoto.com/Peter Zelei

The illustrations for this book were created with black pen,
pencil, and digital media.

Design Element: Shutterstock: Slanapotam

Printed and bound in China.
010377F17

UNICORN RIDERS

Willow's Victory

Aleesah Darlison

Illustrations by
Jill Brailsford

PICTURE WINDOW BOOKS
a capstone imprint

Willow & Obecky

Willow's symbol
- a violet—represents being watchful and faithful

Uniform color
- green

Unicorn
- Obecky has a black opal horn.
- She has the gifts of healing and strength.

Ellabeth & Fayza

Ellabeth's symbol
- a hummingbird—represents energy, persistence, and loyalty

Uniform color
- red

Unicorn
- Fayza has an orange topaz horn.
- She has the gift of speed and can also light the dark with her golden magic.

Quinn & Ula

Quinn's symbol
- a butterfly—represents change and lightness

Uniform color
- blue

Unicorn
- Ula has a ruby horn.
- She has the gift of speaking with Quinn using mind-messages.
- She can also sense danger.

Krystal & Estrella

Krystal's symbol
- a diamond—represents perfection, wisdom, and beauty

Uniform color
- purple

Unicorn
- Estrella has a pearl horn.
- She has the gift of enchantment.

The Unicorn Riders' World

The Unicorn Riders of Avamay

Under the guidance of their leader, Jala, the Unicorn Riders and their magical unicorns protect the Kingdom of Avamay from the threats of evil Lord Valerian.

Decades ago, Lord Valerian forcefully took over the neighboring kingdom of Obeera. He began capturing every magical creature across the eight kingdoms. Luckily, King Perry saved four of Avamay's unicorns. He asked the unicorns to help protect Avamay. And that's when ordinary girls were chosen to be the first Unicorn Riders.

A Rider is chosen when her name and likeness appear in The Choosing Book, which is guarded by Jala. It holds the details of all the past, present, and future Riders. No one can see who the future Riders will be until it is time for a new Rider to be chosen. Only then will The Choosing Book display her details.

CHAPTER 1

WILLOW SPRINTED THROUGH THE field, her legs pumping as she plowed through the long grass. Her lungs felt ready to burst, but she kept going. She was enjoying pushing herself and feeling the blood rush through her veins, hot and fast.

Willow's unicorn, Obecky, whinnied as she trotted beside her Rider. Her black opal horn glinted in the spring sunshine.

"Come on, girl," Willow panted. "Don't go easy on me."

When they reached the riverbank, Willow tore off her boots and tunic top, which was embroidered with her violet symbol. Jala, the Unicorn Riders' leader, had chosen Willow's symbol. It stood for faithfulness and watchfulness, two qualities Willow often used in her role as Head Rider.

Leaving her undershirt and leggings on, Willow dove into the water. Obecky plunged in beside her. Willow swam back and forth across the river until she was exhausted. Surfacing for air, she treaded water. She laughed and splashed Obecky before flipping onto her back with a sigh.

"Ah, this is the life," she said as she floated lazily and stared up at the cloudless blue sky.

Willow was practicing for the upcoming annual Spring Tournament, which the Riders regularly competed in. Any day now, the Unicorn Riders expected a message from Queen Heart approving their trip. Usually, the Riders only traveled on missions for the Queen or to conduct important matters of state. The Spring Tournament was a chance for something different.

As long as there weren't urgent matters to attend to, and as long as Lord Valerian didn't cause any trouble, the Riders would be able to go to the tournament.

Lord Valerian was the evil ruler of the neighboring kingdom of Obeera. For decades he had been starting wars, pitting people and kingdoms against one another, and capturing or destroying magical creatures.

Do evil rulers take holidays? Willow mused. *I sure hope so . .*

The Spring Tournament was held every year to celebrate the new season. Willow had won four events at the last games and was returning as a champion.

"I must win at this tournament, too," Willow told Obecky. "Anything else won't do."

"Well, I hope you're ready for some stiff competition," said a voice.

Willow looked up to see Ellabeth on her unicorn, Fayza. The other Riders, Krystal and Quinn, sat mounted on their unicorns, too.

Willow grinned. "Why's that?" she asked.

"We're going to make you work for those medals," Ellabeth said. "Can't have you getting a big head from winning twice in a row."

Willow laughed. "We'll see about that," she said.

"You're one to talk, Ellabeth," Krystal replied smartly. "Both of you are far too serious about this tournament. It should be fun."

"I agree," said Quinn.

Willow kicked her feet and paddled closer to the bank. "Healthy competition is fun," said Willow. "Don't you want to give it your best shot?"

"Of course we do," Krystal said. "But we also like to enjoy our events."

"You like showing off," Ellabeth teased.

"And you don't?" Krystal said, playfully. "You've been shoving your martial arts medal in my face for a year. If you win again, I bet I'll never hear the end of it."

Ellabeth snorted with laughter. "You're right. I do get carried away," she said.

"That's an understatement," said Krystal.

"So, are you here to watch me swim, or did you have something to tell me?" Willow asked.

"There's a message from the palace," Quinn said. "Jala wants us."

As their leader, Jala was responsible for training and managing the Riders. A girl was chosen to be a Unicorn Rider when her name appeared in The Choosing Book. Although every girl in the kingdom dreamed of becoming a Unicorn Rider, there could only ever be four at a time; one for each unicorn.

"You go, and I'll catch up," Willow said. "I know Jala hates waiting."

The other girls galloped away. As Willow waded out of the river, she stepped on a jagged rock, slicing her heel open. Wincing, she sat down to inspect the cut.

Obecky nickered. Willow glanced

up to see blue-gray magic whirling out from her unicorn's horn.

All unicorns had a special skill. Obecky's was the power to heal and calm. With the tournament looming, Willow had to be fit and healthy. An injured foot was the last thing she needed.

But using Obecky's magic now seemed like cheating. Jala had magic ointment that healed cuts, too. Willow didn't want to use that either. Magic, in any form, wasn't allowed to be used by the competitors, and Willow was determined to go into the tournament fairly.

"Thanks, Obecky, but I'll be fine," Willow said. "It's just a scratch."

Obecky nodded her head, obeying Willow. The magic evaporated.

Willow dressed quickly and rode up to the estate, where she found everyone in the meeting room. Her heel hurt as she walked. She ignored it, thinking the pain would soon fade.

"The message you've been waiting for is finally here," Jala said as Willow sat down. "Queen Heart has given her approval for you to attend the Spring Tournament. And she will be accompanying you."

Excited cheers erupted from the girls.

"When do we leave?" Quinn asked.

"Tomorrow morning," Jala said. "You'll take the unicorns and ride southeast to Lake Feather-Lay. The southern plains will be the perfect place to host this year's tournament."

"That's in Cardamon!" Ellabeth squealed. "I hope my parents come to watch me compete."

"Send word to them when you're nearby," Jala said. "It will be good for you to see them."

"I wish I had parents who could come," Quinn said sadly. Quinn was an orphan. She'd never known her parents.

"Don't worry," Willow said, rushing to Quinn's side. "We'll be your cheer squad."

"For sure," Ellabeth and Krystal agreed.

● CHAPTER 2 ●

JALA; ALDA, THE COOK; and Old Elsid, the groundskeeper, said goodbye to the Riders the next morning.

The girls were dressed in their best uniforms and sat mounted on their unicorns: Willow on Obecky, Quinn on Ula, Krystal on Estrella, and Ellabeth on Fayza.

"I'm sorry I can't come with you," Jala said, "but someone needs to stay here in case anything urgent comes up."

"It's okay. We will fill you in on everything when we get back," Willow promised.

"Make sure you do Avamay proud," Old Elsid said. "And come home with lots of medals."

Krystal laughed. "No pressure or anything," she said.

"Shush, you," Alda said, nudging Old Elsid. "Don't listen to him, Riders. Just do your best. It's not about winning, is it, Jala?"

"No, it's not," Jala agreed. "I'll be proud of them no matter what. So will Queen Heart."

Willow knew Jala meant what she said, but she still couldn't help hoping she would win something. She had always been competitive. "We have a long ride ahead of us before we reach Feather-Lay," Willow said. "We'd best be off. Do we ride as one?"

Just as the Riders were about to reply, the Queen's messenger galloped up. The Riders recognized him instantly from his purple coat and gold sash.

"Honorable Riders!" he cried as his horse skidded to a halt. "I'm glad I caught you."

"What is it?" Willow asked, worried they might be ordered on a last-minute mission.

"Queen Heart wishes to advise that she will be delayed in leaving for the tournament," the messenger said. "Prince Simon is unwell, so she wants to stay with him until he's better."

"Poor Prince Simon," said Quinn, who was close to the prince. "Will he be okay?"

The messenger nodded. "The doctor expects a full recovery, but you know Queen Heart dotes on the boy. She won't leave him," said the messenger. "She's hoping to set out in a few days and still make the finals."

"We understand," Willow said, hiding her disappointment. She had hoped the Queen would watch her compete in all her events. Now that wouldn't happen. "Tell her we look forward to seeing her."

"I also have a confidential message for you," said the messenger as he handed Jala an envelope stamped with the Queen's wax seal, a dancing unicorn.

"Sounds like a mission," Ellabeth said.

"Thank you," Jala told the messenger as he left.

"I wonder what it is," Krystal said.

"Let's have a look and see, shall we?" Jala replied. The Riders crowded around her. She opened the letter and read.

Dear Riders,

Trouble is brewing. Yesterday, I received a threatening letter from an anonymous source. It promised danger, upset, and possible sabotage at the Spring Tournament. It seems whomever wrote this letter wants to keep you Riders busy, perhaps even prevent you from competing. We must not let this happen. Please, keep this information a secret, as I do not wish to ruin the games for the other athletes. You know how much they enjoy competing alongside you all! Instead, use your problem-solving skills to uncover the trouble-maker and prevent whomever it is from doing anything dangerous. I will join you the moment I can. Good luck.

Yours as always,

Queen Heart

"Well, you have a mission, Riders," Jala said. "You must do your best to uncover the identity of the person who sent that threatening letter to Queen Heart. And remember, be careful."

With much discussion and questions still flying among them, the Riders waved goodbye and set out. They traveled quickly with the help of Fayza's speed magic. A mere day after leaving Keydell, they arrived at The Fire Line, a row of volcanoes — some still active — that bordered the Cardamon region where Lake Feather-Lay was located.

The Riders skirted the volcanoes, admiring the fertile plains below. Spring crops flourished. Fields of emerald-green rice shoots and bright orange pumpkins could be seen. Small timber cottages, some raised on stilts, dotted the landscape. Children played in front yards, while dogs, cats, and chickens ran between their legs. Women drew water from wells in preparation for dinner. Men sat in doorways chatting and laughing while they carved miniature stone ornaments, which the area was famous for.

Willow caught Ellabeth staring longingly at the houses and fields.

"Can you see your home from here?" Ellabeth asked.

Ellabeth smiled sadly. She shifted her gaze from the fields to Willow. "No, it's far east of here, but this town looks so similar it makes me homesick," she said.

"I hope your parents come to watch you compete," Quinn said. "I'd love to meet them."

Ellabeth cleared her throat. "I hope they get to meet you girls," she said. "I bet they'll love you as much as I do."

"I hope so," Willow said cheerfully. "We'll send a messenger to their village once we reach the tournament. Speaking of which, I see flags flying." She pointed in the distance and urged Obecky forward. "Last one there has to pitch the tent!"

• CHAPTER 3 •

THE RIDERS SOON ARRIVED at the Spring Tournament. Teams from across the kingdom put up tents, lit campfires, and prepared practice areas. The Riders picked a spot where they could pitch their own tent. When they trotted over to the space, which was near a group of boys who were also competing, they caused a stir. Whispers erupted all around.

"I wasn't sure they'd come," said one boy.

"They come every year, don't they?" someone asked.

"Usually, but you never know what missions they're on," another replied.

"How about those unicorns? They're even more beautiful than the legends say," said one of the boys.

"Honorable Riders," said one boy stepping forward. "We're honored by your presence. Not to mention the great honor it is competing alongside you."

Willow smiled. "That's an awful lot of honoring," she said.

The boy's cheeks flamed red. "I-I'm terribly sorry," he said. "Like most of my friends here, this is my first tournament and the first time I've met Unicorn Riders." He gulped nervously. "I wanted to make a good impression. And now, you must think I'm stupid."

"Of course not," Quinn said. She shook his hand to put him at ease. "But, please, for the tournament, don't think of us as Unicorn Riders. Think of us as friends and fellow athletes. We don't wish to be treated any differently."

"Ah, sure," the boy said. "We'll try. If we can, I mean."

"What's your name?" Krystal asked.

The boy groaned. "My apologies for my poor manners, again," he said. "My name is Raleg."

"You look like you're from Cardamon," Ellabeth said. "I grew up there."

"We're all from Cardamon," Raleg said as he gestured to the boys crowding behind him. "What an honor it is competing with a Rider from our own region."

Several boys elbowed him. "They said no more honoring, Raleg," the boys said.

Raleg slapped his forehead. "Sorry," he said. "This could take some getting used to. How about I show you around?"

"That would be great," Willow said. "Are the unicorns safe here?"

Raleg's companions hurried forward, vying for attention. "They'll be safe with us," said the boys. "We can feed and water them for you."

"Just let them graze," Willow said. "Don't do anything silly. Okay? Like trying to ride them."

Willow was wary about leaving the unicorns with strangers, especially with a potential saboteur at the tournament.

"No, of course not. We would never," the boys assured her.

The Riders followed Raleg on a tour of the tournament grounds. Areas had been marked out for jousting, hurling, sprints, archery, gymnastics, falconry, and several other events. A stadium had even been built for spectators.

They saw a girl practicing at the archery targets. She looked Willow's age. She was tall and gangly with a thick auburn braid snaking down her back. She had excellent aim and hit the target squarely each time.

"Who's that?" Krystal asked.

Willow could tell she was stunned by the girl's accuracy. Archery was Krystal's best event.

Looks like Krystal's discovered some tough competition already, Willow thought. *I wonder if I will, too?*

"That's Felina Farrow," Raleg said, his voice breaking through Willow's thoughts. "She's from up north, near Trilby. She is sponsored by Sir Drexitt. She's amazing at everything."

"Farrow. Why is that name familiar?" Quinn asked.

"Her brother is a past champion," Raleg said. "Haven't heard about him in a while though. Don't know what happened to him."

"She's very pretty," Krystal observed.

"I hadn't noticed," Raleg said.

Ellabeth grinned. "Sure you hadn't," she teased.

"Yes, well," Raleg coughed. "Let's move on."

They saw a boy practicing with the pell. The pell was a wooden post planted firmly in the ground and used as a target for sword practice. The swords used for the tournament were made of light timber. They weren't the real thing.

The boy had long, tangled black hair. His clothes, though clean, were faded and tattered and not at all like the other competitors'. Jagged scars ran down one of his legs. His face was scarred, too.

Those scars look frightening, Willow thought. *So do his sword skills.*

"Who's that?" Quinn asked.

"Marlow Grimm," Raleg replied.

"Unfortunate name," Ellabeth said.

"Unfortunate-looking boy," Willow murmured. "What do you know about him, Raleg?"

"Not much," Raleg said. "He only arrived yesterday. By himself."

"Where's he from?" Krystal asked.

"Obeera, apparently," replied Raleg.

Willow grimaced. "I didn't think Obeerians were allowed to compete in Avamay's Spring Tournament," Willow said.

Raleg shrugged. "He paid his fee like everyone else," said Raleg. "But he has no supporters and no other team members. He's going to find this tournament difficult." Raleg waved to someone in the distance. "Excuse me, Riders, I must practice for my events."

The moment Raleg departed, the Riders gathered close to talk privately.

"Why would a boy like Marlow come here?" Ellabeth asked.

"Same reason everyone's here," Quinn said. "To win prizes and get noticed. If he does well, one of the lords may employ him or train him as a soldier. This tournament could set him up for life."

"He's got guts, that's for sure," Krystal said.

"And he looks like a dangerous rival," Willow added. "I'm worried that if he's from Obeera he's working for Valerian. And that he could be the saboteur."

"What if he's not?" Quinn countered. "What if he's innocent? And friendly?"

"I guess we'll soon find out, won't we?" Willow replied.

• CHAPTER 4 •

WILLOW'S FEET POUNDED THE dirt path. Her heart thudded in her chest. Sweat dripped down her forehead.

She'd been running for ages and was starting to tire. The cut on her heel was throbbing again. Every step sent pain shooting up her leg.

I'll look at it later, she thought. *It's a shame I can't use Obecky's magic to fix it, but that's the way I wanted it. Using magic will get me disqualified from the games. And I'm not about to let that happen.*

Willow peeked over her shoulder. She couldn't see anyone.

Keep going, she told herself. *Almost there.*

The cross-country race was a test of stamina and endurance. The course snaked through the forest and over a hill. Willow couldn't see over the top yet, but she knew she was near the finish. She just had to hang on.

Through the trees ahead, she caught a flash of movement. It was Marlow Grimm, leading the race. Willow was in second place.

Come on, you can do it, she urged herself. *Push hard.*

Hearing footsteps behind her, she glanced around to see Felina Farrow.

Where did she come from? Willow wondered. *Last time I saw her, she was way back.*

"Hey, there," Felina said as she glided past Willow. "Pretty tough course, huh?"

Felina didn't have a hair out of place. Nor was she sweating.

How does she do that? Willow thought as she watched Felina speed ahead.

Willow had to cling on to her position. Otherwise she'd miss out on making it into the finals. Only the top three athletes from each heat continued on. She had to make Avamay proud. She had to make the other Unicorn Riders proud.

Over the last three days, the other Riders had all made it to the finals in one event or another. Ellabeth in martial arts and fencing. Krystal in archery. Quinn in gymnastics. Willow couldn't let the team down. She'd missed out on a finals place in her other events. It all came down to the cross-country race.

My sore foot has been holding me back, Willow thought. *I can't let that continue.*

Not only that, but the Riders had so far been unable to discover the saboteur. Yesterday, they had found a note pinned to their tent. It said that since the Queen wasn't coming to the tournament, the Riders had better beware.

Get ready for mischief, the note said. You will take notice of me.

Willow shuddered. This tournament would be a disaster on all counts if she didn't get things together. Starting with this race.

Cresting the hill, Willow saw the finish line. Felina was closing in on Marlow. The pack was closing in on Willow.

A huge crowd was gathered. All the teams and their supporters were watching the race, cheering madly. Some were waving flags and banners.

Legs burning, heart pounding, Willow forced herself to keep going.

Marlow and Felina were neck and neck as they sprinted toward the finish line. Three boys behind Willow tried to jostle past her. Willow scanned the crowd for the Riders. They waved to her and cheered. With a smile of determination, she looked back in time to see Marlow push Felina.

That's not nice! she thought.

Felina stumbled but kept her feet. Marlow crossed the finish line, followed by Felina. Willow made it into third place, barely beating a tumble of boys and girls.

Quinn, Krystal, and Ellabeth ran over and offered Willow a flask of water. The unicorns trotted up behind.

"Well done," Krystal said. "Third place!"

Willow couldn't help feeling disappointed. She'd expected to do much better. She would have her work cut out for her if she wanted to win the final.

"Great race," Felina congratulated her. "You had me there for a while. I actually thought you Riders would be too busy with your missions to attend the tournament. I'm glad you still found time to be here."

"We always find time for the Spring Tournament," Willow puffed as she tried to get her breath back. "You ran well. Pity Marlow pushed you."

Felina's face suddenly clouded. "Marlow Grimm is a troublemaker," she said.

Willow exchanged glances with the other Riders. "In what way?" asked Willow.

"He's mean and nasty," Felina said. "I wouldn't be surprised if he's cheated in other events, too."

"He doesn't seem one bit sorry," Ellabeth said, nodding toward Marlow, who was standing alone. No one had run over to congratulate him. He caught the girls looking and glared.

Willow marched over to him. "You shouldn't have pushed Felina," she said. "You could have hurt her."

"You're quick to take her side," Marlow said. "I thought Unicorn Riders were fair and just."

Willow was shocked. "We are," she said. "I know what I saw. And I think I should report you. I could get you disqualified."

"She pushed me first," Marlow said. "Report me if you want. I don't care." He strode off, shaking his head.

"I don't like that boy," Willow fumed. "He's far too arrogant."

"He looks like he's had a hard life," Quinn said gently. "He's alone here, too. Imagine how he feels."

"But he cheated," Willow insisted.

"Then why didn't the judges pick it up?" Ellabeth asked.

"Maybe they didn't see it," Krystal said.

"Don't worry," Felina said smiling. "I'll beat him in the final. You'll see."

She sure is confident, Willow thought. *Doesn't she think I can beat her?*

"I'm still worried he's working for Valerian," Willow said. "I don't trust him."

"Really?" Felina said, her eyes lighting up.

Willow hesitated. "Sorry. I forgot where I was for a minute," she said.

"No problem. I'll, er, leave you alone," Felina said as she wandered off.

"Oops," Willow said, cringing. "I wish I hadn't said that."

"I'm sure we can trust Felina," Quinn said. "From what I've seen of her, she seems nice."

"You think everyone is nice," Ellabeth said.

Quinn blushed. "There's nothing wrong with seeing the good in people," she said.

"I guess not," Ellabeth said, laughing. "Anyway, if Marlow is working for Valerian, I don't think he'd waste his time sending him to the Spring Tournament. What's he got to gain by that?"

"Valerian likes making our lives difficult," Krystal said. "We're looking for a saboteur, remember? That person could easily be Marlow, with Valerian behind him. He is Obeerian, after all."

"Raleg said Marlow doesn't live in Obeera any more," Quinn said.

"That could be a story he's spinning," Willow countered. "Either way, he makes me suspicious. I wonder how he got those scars?"

"I don't know," Ellabeth said, "but I'd sure like to find out."

"Me, too," Willow agreed. "Which is precisely what I intend on doing. And if Marlow Grimm is the saboteur, I aim to stop him before he does anything dangerous."

"There haven't been any sabotage attempts yet," Quinn pointed out. "What if this is all a hoax?"

"It could be a hoax," Willow agreed. "Or perhaps whoever is responsible is biding their time, waiting to strike. Looks like we have some investigating to do."

● CHAPTER 5 ●

WILLOW'S HEAT HAD BEEN the last event of the day. Now the competitors had free time to do what they liked.

"Felina invited us to go swimming earlier," Ellabeth told Willow. "Do you want to come, too?"

"No thanks," Willow replied. She'd been feeling troubled since her race. "I don't feel like it."

"A swim might soothe your tired muscles," Quinn said.

Krystal agreed. "You want to make sure you're fully recovered for the final," she said.

"I will be," Willow said. "I just don't feel like a swim. You girls go. Don't worry about me."

"Hey, Riders." Felina waved, walking up. "Ready for that swim?"

"We sure are," Krystal said.

"Fabulous," Felina said. She turned to Willow. "You're not coming?"

Willow shook her head.

"Can we take the unicorns?" Felina asked, eyeing the animals grazing on the long, succulent grass. "It seems a shame not to show them off."

"They're not meant for showing off," Willow said.

"Oh, yes, of course," Felina replied hurriedly. "I didn't mean anything by it. Still, they could do with a walk after eating this rich grass."

Krystal appealed to Willow. "A walk to the lake won't hurt, will it?" she asked. "We'll be with them the whole time."

"I guess not," Willow conceded. She couldn't see the harm in letting the unicorns go. Not with the Riders to protect them. "Sure, you take them."

"What about Obecky?" Quinn asked.

"Thanks, but I'll watch her," Willow replied.

Laughing and chatting, the Riders grabbed their towels and headed to the lake with Felina. Willow felt a pang of guilt by not going.

It was my choice, she reminded herself.

Willow sat beneath the shade of an oak tree. She picked up her sketchbook and began drawing the wildflowers she saw in the field. But she couldn't concentrate.

Marlow Grimm was on her mind.

Is he dangerous? she wondered. *Does he work for Lord Valerian? Now might be a good time to find out.*

Snapping her sketchbook shut, Willow stood up. When she put weight on her foot, pain shot up her leg. She dropped to the ground and slid her boot off. A puffy, pink lump throbbed on her heel. When she pressed it, the pain was unbearable. "Ouch!" she gasped. "It's infected."

Again, Willow considered using Obecky's magic. But she quickly dismissed the idea. Other athletes probably had injuries also, yet they didn't have access to magic. She shouldn't either. Not for the tournament. Besides, if she used magic and others found out, she'd be disqualified.

Imagine how disappointed Jala would be, she told herself.

Carefully, Willow pulled her boot back on and then called Obecky.

"Let's go for a ride," Willow said to Obecky. "I want to do some investigating."

Obecky nickered, flicking her tail in agitation. Willow hesitated. Obecky was usually so calm.

"What's wrong, girl?" Willow asked. Her neck hairs pricked. She scanned the trees and spotted Marlow.

At least I don't have to go far to find my suspect, she thought.

"What are you doing?" Willow asked.

Marlow scowled as he slunk out of the forest. "Nothing," he said.

"Were you watching me?" Willow asked.

"No," he replied.

Willow glanced at Obecky and then back at Marlow. "You were watching Obecky," she said. "Weren't you?"

"No crime in looking," Marlow said.

Marlow was right. Looking at unicorns wasn't forbidden. Everyone was fascinated by them. But if Marlow was working for Valerian, maybe he was here to steal the unicorns. Willow knew Valerian wanted to get his hands on them. He'd tried several times before.

"Keep away from the unicorns, okay?" Willow said.

"Whatever you say, Honorable Rider," Marlow said. His words dripped with sarcasm.

Willow flinched. She'd hoped to talk to Marlow to discover more about him. To perhaps uncover any plot he had planned.

This wasn't going so well.

"That came out wrong," Willow said in a softened voice. "I guess you're just curious. You've probably never seen unicorns before."

"Don't worry," Marlow grunted. "I'm not interested in your precious unicorns. They're too fancy for me. You Riders aren't what you're cracked up to be either."

Willow's temper flared at the insult.

"You'd better watch yourself, Marlow Grimm," she snapped, before mounting Obecky and cantering away.

She hadn't gone far when screams made her stop.

"That sounds like trouble," she said. Willow turned Obecky toward the lake, where the screams came from.

As they galloped closer, Willow saw three heads bobbing above the water. She recognized Quinn's bright red curls and Ellabeth's dark hair. The other girl wasn't Krystal though. It was Felina.

Where's Krystal? Willow wondered.

Ula, Fayza, and Estrella were on the banks of the lake. Estrella pranced about nervously and whinnied pitifully.

"Get out of the water!" Felina shouted. "There's something in here."

Felina, Quinn, and Ellabeth swam for the shore.

Obecky came to a halt. "Where's Krystal?" Willow asked.

Ellabeth stumbled onto the banks, dripping wet and trembling. Her face was as pale as an eggshell. Willow had never seen her so frightened.

"She's disappeared!" said Quinn.

● CHAPTER 6 ●

WILLOW LEAPED OFF OBECKY and sprinted toward the water, ignoring the pain in her foot.

"Don't go in," Felina warned. "Something touched me. I think it bit Krystal."

"She's my friend," Willow said. "I can't leave her. What's in there?"

"I'm not sure," Felina said. She looked as worried as Ellabeth. "Maybe a water snake. She went under so fast, I lost her."

Willow's mind worked methodically. "Ellabeth, tell Fayza to use her light magic," said Willow. "It's deep and dark down there, and it's stopping us from seeing Krystal."

Ellabeth instructed Fayza to place her horn on the lake's surface. Light radiated out across the water then seeped down. The Riders examined the depths.

"There!" Quinn shouted. "I see her."

Krystal's lifeless body hung suspended deep beneath the water. Her long, golden hair floated around her.

Willow quickly tugged off her boots and tunic top.

"Can I help?" Felina asked.

"No. Wait here. I'll get her," Willow said.

Ula's magic whirled as she mind-messaged Quinn. "Ula says she isn't breathing," Quinn said. "Hurry, Willow!"

Willow dove into the lake and swam down to Krystal. She plunged deeper and deeper, desperate to reach her friend.

50

Krystal was a long way down. Willow was in danger of running out of breath. She kicked harder and stretched her long arms and fingers to grasp Krystal. Then she powered up to the surface, dragging Krystal with her. Quinn and Ellabeth ran into the water to help haul their friend out.

Felina wrung her hands. "Is she all right?" she asked.

Krystal's face was ghostly pale. Her lips were blue. She didn't move.

"I don't know yet," Willow said.

"Quick, Willow!" Quinn urged. "Ula says her heart isn't beating."

The Riders kneeled beside Krystal. Onlookers crowded around, including Raleg and his friends.

Willow checked Krystal for bite marks, but it was impossible to see with people standing over her and blocking the light.

"Please," Willow appealed to Raleg. "Will you have everyone move back."

"Of course," Raleg said, shooing the gawkers away.

"Obecky?" Willow said, trying not to panic. "Where are you?"

"Everyone move back!" Ellabeth shouted. "Can't you see my friend's in trouble? Move back."

Quinn squeezed Ellabeth's shoulder. "Stay calm," she said gently. "You can't help Krystal if you're upset."

Willow heard a nicker. The crowd parted to let Obecky through.

"If ever there was a time we needed your magic, Obecky, it's now," said Willow. "Please, revive her. You're her only hope."

Obecky lowered her horn toward Krystal's unmoving chest. Gray-blue magic swirled around Krystal's body, weaving over her chest and into her mouth and nose and seeping into her heart and lungs. Soon, Krystal's entire body was wrapped in magic like a caterpillar in a cocoon.

The onlookers gasped in wonder. It wasn't every day they saw unicorn magic at work.

The Riders watched and waited.

After a few moments, Krystal's eyelids began to flutter.

"Something's happening," Ellabeth said, her eyes shining with hope. "Please, let her be okay."

Water gushed from Krystal's mouth. With a cough and a splutter she sat up, gasped, and then fell back onto the ground, unconscious.

"No, no, no!" Ellabeth said, tugging at her hair. "This can't be happening."

"What's wrong?" Quinn asked. She looked at Willow. "Why isn't she waking up?"

Willow didn't know what to do. Obecky's magic had cleared the water from Krystal's lungs, but it hadn't properly revived her. *What was wrong?* she wondered.

She clutched Krystal's hand. "Krystal, can you hear me?" Willow asked.

Krystal groaned. She opened her eyes, gazing at the sea of faces above her. "Why is everyone staring at me?" she asked.

"You're alive!" Willow exclaimed, hugging her. Quinn and Ellabeth followed, wiping away tears.

The crowd cheered.

Willow stood up. "Everyone, you can go now," she said. "Krystal is going to be fine."

Reluctantly, people turned to leave.

"Can I get her anything?" Felina asked.

"No. We'll take her back to our campsite," Willow said. "But you can tell me what happened."

"There was something in the lake," Felina said. "Like I said, I think it was a water snake. It touched my leg. I think it bit Krystal. It all happened in an instant."

"I didn't find any bite marks on her," Willow said. "Krystal, do you remember being bitten?"

Her hair was dripping wet, and her face was green with sickness. "I can't remember," she said rubbing her forehead. "My mind's too fuzzy. I need to rest."

"Good idea," Willow said. "I'll help you back to our camp."

"I'll take Krystal's unicorn if you like," someone offered.

Willow glanced up to see Marlow. *Him again,* she thought crossly. *And he's interested in Estrella, too.*

"Thanks, but we'll look after her," Willow said. She wasn't about to let anyone near the unicorns, especially after Krystal's scare. "It's best Estrella stays with Krystal right now."

"I was only trying to help," Marlow said. "Estrella looks distressed. I thought I could calm her down. I know plenty about horses."

"Estrella is a unicorn, not a horse," Willow snapped. "They're two vastly different creatures. You being near Estrella will only make her more anxious. If you really want to help, find out what hurt Krystal."

• CHAPTER 7 •

BY THE TIME THEY got Krystal back to the camp, her teeth were chattering, and her body was shaking uncontrollably.

"What's wrong with me?" she whimpered.

"I'm not sure," Willow said. "Maybe something in the water is making you sick."

"Lake Feather-Lay has the purest water in Avamay," Quinn said. "This doesn't make sense."

"I agree," Willow said, chewing on her lip. "But right now I'm more concerned about getting Krystal dry and comfortable."

Willow noticed Felina hovering. She wished she would go away, but she didn't want to offend her.

Instead, she focused on Krystal. She lowered her onto a stretcher bed outside their tent to give her fresh air.

"Should we use Obecky's magic again?" Ellabeth asked.

"A little more can't hurt," Willow said.

"You used magic before at the lake, too," Felina pointed out. "That means Krystal is disqualified from the tournament."

"Looks like you've got a clear shot at the archery title then," Ellabeth said.

"I didn't mean it like that," Felina said, blushing.

"If Krystal misses an event, so be it," Willow said. "These are special circumstances. We can't risk our friend's life for the sake of a competition."

Krystal was too ill to argue.

Willow prompted Obecky to help Krystal once more.

The unicorn spun her magic over the sick girl. Krystal's tense body relaxed. Color flared in her cheeks. But she remained weak.

"Get her dry clothes and blankets," Willow instructed Quinn, who hurried off.

"Do you think it's shock?" Ellabeth asked.

Willow shook her head. "It's more than that," said Willow. "This is some mystery illness or dark magic. Not even Obecky's powers can overcome it."

Quinn returned with a fresh uniform and blankets for Krystal. The Riders discreetly changed her and tucked the blankets over her.

"Should we move her inside the tent?" Quinn asked.

"No," Willow replied. "It's too cramped in there. We can care for her better out here."

Marlow strode up carrying an armload of wood. "I thought you might need some firewood," he explained. "It will be dark soon, and a fire will warm her. A hot meal might help, too."

"We can look after her ourselves," Willow said.

Quinn touched her arm. "He's trying to help," she said.

"A fire is an excellent idea," Ellabeth said as she held Krystal's hand. "Her lips are still so blue despite the blankets. She looks frozen to death."

Willow paused. Quinn and Ellabeth were right. Marlow did seem genuinely worried for Krystal. Or was she mistaking guilt for concern? She couldn't tell.

"Thank you, Marlow," Willow said. She gave him the benefit of the doubt. For now. "A fire would be wonderful. Can you start it for us?"

Overhead, a familiar screech sounded.

"It's Belmont," Quinn said.

Belmont was the Queen's messenger falcon. He screeched again, circling Willow before landing on her outstretched arm.

Willow untied the message cylinder from around the falcon's leg and unraveled the note. "Prince Simon is better, so Queen Heart is on her way to the tournament," said Willow. "She's coming via Old

Valley Road by coach tomorrow. Unescorted. She wants to keep her visit low-key."

"That's a quiet road," Ellabeth said. "Hardly anyone travels it."

Willow caught a flicker of something in Felina's eyes. She frowned, wondering whether she should ask the other girl to leave. Felina seemed friendly and helpful. It was hard to think bad of her. And yet, something told Willow they shouldn't be discussing the Queen's movements so freely in front of outsiders.

"Let's hope Krystal has recovered by then," Quinn said as she smoothed her friend's hair from her face. "Queen Heart will be upset if she sees her like this."

Night fell with Krystal dropping in and out of consciousness. The unicorns lingered nearby. Estrella paced up and down as she watched her Rider.

Willow sat with Krystal, refusing to leave. Felina left, and Quinn led a reluctant Ellabeth off to bed to rest. Marlow stayed with Willow, insisting on bringing more firewood.

"Don't you have someplace to go?" Willow asked him.

"No," he replied.

"Why did you come to the tournament alone?" she asked.

"Why not?" Marlow countered.

"Because athletes usually come sponsored or with a team. You have neither," Willow said.

"Thanks for reminding me," Marlow said, laughing as he plucked a grass stem to chew on. "No Avamayans will sponsor an Obeerian kid. I'm an outsider; you know that. I wasn't exactly going to ask Lord Valerian to sponsor me, either."

Willow blinked the sleepiness from her eyes. She sat up. Was she finally going to learn the truth about Marlow? "How come?" Willow asked.

"He's the reason I left Obeera," said Marlow.

"Why? What happened?" asked Willow.

"Same thing that happened to thousands of Obeerians who have tried to stand against Valerian,"

Marlow explained. "My father was an outspoken writer. He printed articles and pamphlets about Valerian, encouraging Obeerians to overthrow him. Valerian hunted him down and killed him, my mother, and my two brothers. I escaped. But not without a few souvenirs to show for it." He indicated his leg and face.

Quinn was right, Willow thought. *He has had a hard life. Does that make him a bad person?*

"How did you get the scars?" Willow asked.

"Valerian's men set wolves on me," Marlow said.

Willow gasped. "That's awful!" she said.

"A friend of my father's arrived just in time," said Marlow. "He chased the wolves away and saved my life." Marlow stared into the fire, remembering. His eyes flicked up to meet Willow's. For the first time, she noticed how striking they were. If it wasn't for the scars and tangled hair, Marlow would be handsome. Willow stopped herself. Was she changing her opinion of him?

"I almost died from the infection," Marlow continued. "Once I recovered, I left Obeera and never returned. For the last two years, I've been living in Bella Plains, north of here, and earning my keep as a farmhand. But I have bigger plans. That's why I've come to the tournament."

"How did you get here?" asked Willow.

"I walked," said Marlow

"That's a long way," Willow said.

Marlow shrugged. "Walking never hurt anyone," he replied.

"It must have taken weeks," said Willow.

Marlow nodded.

Willow was impressed. Surely anyone with that much determination had earned their place at the tournament. No matter where they were born.

Have I been wrong about Marlow? she thought. *Can he be trusted?*

"Did Felina really push you in the race today?" Willow asked.

"I said she did, didn't I?" he replied.

"But she seems so . . . nice," said Willow. "Friendly and gentle, like she wouldn't hurt anyone."

Marlow snorted. "Trust me, Felina will do anything to win," he said. "Even take out the competition." He nodded toward Krystal. "Aren't you suspicious about what happened at the lake?"

"I have had doubts," said Willow. "Do you think Felina's involved somehow?"

"Krystal's archery skills are renowned," Marlow said. "The other athletes know how badly Felina wants to beat her. She wants to win that event as much as she wants to win the cross-country race."

"But why?" asked Willow.

"I don't know," he said. "Maybe to be recognized as a champion? Maybe to get noticed by the Queen?"

Ice splashed through Willow's veins. Could that be it? Could Felina be the saboteur? The one who promised mischief and destruction? Krystal was out of the archery event, clearing the way for Felina to win the medal. That medal would earn her an audience with the Queen. If Felina was the saboteur, who knows what might happen if she got close to the Queen?

Willow's mind raced with the possibilities, but she couldn't let on to Marlow.

"You're being paranoid," Willow said, waving him away. "Felina's not like that."

Marlow leaned close. "Oh? How well do you know her?" he asked.

• CHAPTER 8 •

A TWIG SNAPPED IN the darkness. Willow held a finger to her lips.

"Hey there," a voice called. Felina appeared. She saw Marlow and pulled a face. "Oh. You're here."

"Don't worry," Marlow muttered. "I'm leaving." He rose and stalked off.

"You should be careful who you talk to," Felina said after he'd gone. "That Obeerian boy is trouble."

Had Felina been listening to her and Marlow talking? Willow hoped not. And why was Felina up so late? Was Marlow right about her? Should Willow be suspicious of Felina?

Willow didn't know who to trust any more.

"I'm warming to him actually," Willow said. She smiled, studying Felina's face for a reaction.

From what Willow could tell, the other girl gave nothing away.

Just then, Ellabeth and Quinn wandered over.

"We were too worried to sleep," Ellabeth said. She yawned as she and Quinn sat down. "How is she?"

"She's showing no improvement," Willow said, frowning. "Despite Obecky's magic."

"It's a shame Krystal can't compete in the tournament any longer," Felina said. "But she's lucky to have friends like you. I wish I was a Rider."

Willow laughed. "You and every other girl we meet," she said.

"I meant it as a compliment," Felina said, biting her lip.

"I'm sorry," Willow said truthfully. "I wasn't trying to make you feel bad."

"That's okay," said Felina. "Is it as wonderful as everyone thinks?"

"Everything you've ever heard and more," Quinn said.

"It's also a lot of hard work," Ellabeth added. "And dangerous."

Felina's eyes glowed as she warmed her hands by the fire. "What's the most dangerous mission you've ever been on?" Felina asked.

Before Ellabeth could reply, Willow silenced her with a cautious look.

"We can't talk about it," Willow said.

"Of course," Felina said, seeming disappointed. "I understand. Do you get to see the Queen a lot?"

That's a strange question, Willow thought. *Why her sudden interest in the Queen?*

Marlow stepped back into the firelight. He was carrying a wooden bowl. "I've made something to help Krystal," he said.

"What could be better than unicorn magic?" Ellabeth asked. "It's very powerful."

"Your unicorn magic doesn't seem to be doing much good," Marlow observed. "Krystal's still sick. I found some herbs in the woods. Hyssop and peppermint. They're good for curing chills."

"Where did you learn about herbs?" Quinn asked.

"My mother taught me. And her mother taught her," Marlow said.

"Thanks," Willow said. "We might try them when Krystal wakes next."

"Why not now?" Marlow pressed.

"Please, we know what we're doing," Willow said. "You can go now. We'll take care of Krystal our way."

Marlow's eyes hardened. "Fine. I'll go," he said. He shot Felina a searing glance as he sat the bowl down and strode off.

"Did you see the way he glared at me?" Felina asked. "He's trouble, all right. I bet he's the one sabotaging the tournament."

Willow perked up. How could Felina know about the sabotage plot? The Riders hadn't mentioned it to anyone. Either Felina had been snooping on their private conversations or she knew something. Willow needed to press Felina and dig a little deeper.

"Who said anything about sabotage?" Willow asked.

Felina's cheeks instantly burned red. "Haven't there been rumors?" she quickly replied.

"Not as far as I know. What have you heard?" asked Willow.

Krystal suddenly stirred.

"Oh good, she's waking," Quinn said. "We can ask her what happened at the lake."

Felina squirmed, looking worried. "She'll be too ill for that, surely," said Felina.

"You can never underestimate Krystal," Ellabeth said. "She bounces back pretty well."

Krystal groaned. "Where am I?"

"You're at the Spring Tournament. You're safe," said Willow.

"Where's Estrella?" Krystal asked.

"Right here," Ellabeth said as she led the unicorn over.

"That's better." Krystal sighed, patting Estrella's slender nose.

"Why don't we try Marlow's herbal drink?" Quinn suggested. "It might give Krystal that extra lift she needs to get back on her feet."

Willow turned to look for the bowl.

Felina was holding it. "You read my mind," Felina said, beaming. "I hope Marlow's concoction is okay. Are you sure you want to give it to her?"

Willow nodded. She took the bowl and held it to Krystal's lips.

"Mmm. Tastes delicious," Krystal said. Then suddenly, the color drained from Krystal's face. She fell back, unconscious.

"What happened?" Ellabeth asked. Her face was etched with worry.

"Marlow's herbs have made her worse," Quinn gasped.

Willow felt Krystal's wrist. "Her pulse is beating strongly enough," said Willow. "Maybe she's just sleeping. Her reaction to the herbs was rather unusual though."

"Perhaps Marlow poisoned her," Felina suggested.

"Should we question him?" Quinn said. "Just to make sure he didn't?"

"I'll go," Willow said. "You two stay with Krystal." She glanced sideways at Felina before continuing in a whisper. "Do not take your eyes off Krystal. If her condition changes in any way, come and get me."

• CHAPTER 9 •

WILLOW FOUND MARLOW SITTING by a campfire on the edge of the tournament grounds. He was staring into the fire as he roasted a rabbit in the flames. The delicious smell of cooking meat made Willow's mouth water. She hadn't eaten for hours and was starving.

"I need to speak to you," Willow said.

Marlow nearly dropped the rabbit into the fire. He jumped to his feet. "Willow. What is it?" he asked.

"What did you put in the mixture you gave Krystal?" Willow asked.

"I told you. Hyssop and peppermint. Did you give it to her?" Marlow asked.

"Yes, and now she's worse than ever," said Willow.

"That shouldn't be," Marlow said. "I mixed it myself. Just as my mother would have. Did anyone interfere with it?"

"Why would they do that?" Willow asked.

Marlow shrugged. "I don't know," he said.

Willow stepped closer.

"Are you limping?" Marlow asked.

"That's none of your concern," Willow snapped.

"I might be able to help," he said.

Willow considered showing Marlow her foot, but changed her mind. Just when she had started to like him, Felina had sewn seeds of doubt in her mind.

Who knows what harmful potion he might offer me? she wondered.

"I didn't come to talk about my foot," she said. "I came to find out what you put in your so-called herbal remedy."

"I swear I did nothing wrong," Marlow said, as he took the skewered rabbit from the fire. He sat it on a wooden plate and tore chunks of steaming meat off, wiggling his fingers every so often to cool them. "Would you like something to eat? I caught this myself." He handed her the plate. Willow could see it was the only one he had. She could also see he was trying to please her.

"No, thanks. I'm not hungry," she said.

"But you are stubborn," Marlow said. His eyes danced. Again, Willow marveled at how unusual they were. "Are you really not hungry or are you afraid I'll poison you, too?"

"What do you mean 'too'?" Willow asked.

Marlow sighed. "You're telling the story," he said.

"All I know is that Krystal had a bad reaction to your herbs," Willow said.

"Are you naturally this suspicious of everyone? Or is it because I look different? Because of the . . . scars?" Marlow asked.

Willow stared at the ground, scuffing her boot in the dirt. "It's not that," she protested, although this wasn't entirely true. From the moment she'd first seen him, Willow had judged Marlow because of his scars and because of where he'd been born.

What if I was wrong? she wondered.

"Sure it isn't," said Marlow. "Which is why you can't look me square in the eyes right now." He laughed bitterly. "You expect me to believe you? I see the way people stare at me. I know they're afraid or disgusted because of how I look. It's not my fault. I told you that."

Willow heard the pleading in Marlow's voice. Filled with sympathy for him, she lifted her head to meet his gaze. "Does it upset you?" she asked. "What happened to you?"

"Yes! I mean, no," he said, throwing his hands up. "I don't know. Life goes on. A few scars haven't stopped me from growing tall and strong. Now I'm one of the fastest boys around. You've seen how I run. I can't complain."

Willow sat on a boulder and crossed her arms. "I don't know what to believe anymore," she said.

Marlow thrust the plate of rabbit at her. "Eat," he said.

Unable to resist any longer, Willow ate. The meat was warm, tender, and juicy. Marlow helped himself to the remainder of the rabbit still skewered on the roasting stick. "Maybe it's time you saw past these scars and my Obeerian background to the real me." He jabbed his chest. "I'm a good person, Willow. I don't cheat. I don't hurt others. You can trust me."

He seems so sincere, Willow thought. *Perhaps he is telling the truth. What if Felina did push him? What if someone tampered with his herbal drink?*

Realization struck Willow. Felina had handed her the bowl.

Did Felina put something in the drink while her back was turned? It was possible. And yet, Willow had a hard time believing a friendly, pleasant girl like Felina would cheat or hurt others.

Willow racked her brains, trying to solve the mystery. Who was guilty and who was innocent?

"Thank heavens I've found you!" Ellabeth said, bursting into the ring of firelight. "You'll never guess what Felina's found."

● CHAPTER 10 ●

WILLOW AND THE OTHER Riders studied the damaged equipment scattered on the ground. Broken bows and arrows, mangled targets, shattered pell swords, jousting sticks, and more lay everywhere.

"Who did this?" Willow asked.

"We hoped you could tell us," a tournament official said. "This shed is kept locked, but we found the lock snapped and the equipment destroyed."

"This could end the tournament," Felina said.

"What are we going to do?" Ellabeth asked. "The finals are tomorrow."

"Can we make more equipment?" Willow asked.

"That would take months," the official said. "It's all expertly made."

"We could delay the tournament," Quinn suggested.

"Everything is planned," Willow said, firmly. "Besides, we can't let whoever did this win. Queen Heart arrives tomorrow. We must ensure she has a tournament to watch. Let's see if each team will donate their personal equipment to use. We can still make this happen."

"What about catching the villains who did this?" the official said. "Do you know who it is?"

"Each time something bad happened, the same person was right there," Willow said. "Who caused the fuss with Marlow in the cross-country race?"

"Felina," Ellabeth said.

"Fuss? What do you mean?" Felina asked.

"And who was with Krystal when she almost drowned?" Willow asked.

"Felina," Quinn replied, glancing at her.

"And this evening, who found the damaged equipment?" Willow asked.

"Felina," Ellabeth said.

"I was passing by," Felina argued. "What exactly are you saying, Willow?"

"I thought it was strange when you caught up to me in the cross-country race," Willow said. "You weren't sweating. Your hair was tidy. You even had energy to chat."

"I'm fit," Felina said. "I've been training for months."

"Maybe you have been," Willow said as she paced up and down. *That girl is always coming up with excuses,* she thought. *Or are they lies?* She stopped pacing and faced Felina. "Or maybe something else is going on."

The official looked bewildered. "Like what?" he asked.

"Yes, like what?" Felina demanded. "I'd like to see you prove anything."

"Give me time and perhaps I will," Willow murmured.

"Good luck," Felina huffed before stalking off.

"Wow, she's mad," Ellabeth said.

Willow nodded. "I didn't like doing that, but I wanted to see her reaction," said Willow. "She looked guilty if you ask me. We'll leave it for now, see what happens next. Right now we've got work to do."

The Riders spent hours collecting new equipment. They were talking to Raleg when shouts sounded in the night.

"Stop him! Stop him!" came a voice.

Through the darkness, Marlow came running. Felina was right behind him.

"I've found the saboteur!" she screamed. "He confessed everything. Catch the Obeerian before he escapes."

Marlow froze.

Officials yelled and shook their fists. "Catch him!" they yelled.

For a brief moment, Marlow locked eyes with Willow. Then he turned and fled.

"What should we do?" the officials asked.

Willow wasn't sure if Marlow was guilty, but fleeing hadn't helped his cause. Either way, Willow wanted to be the one to catch him.

"Leave Marlow to us," she told the officials. "You finish collecting the equipment. Remember, everything must be in order for Queen Heart. Quinn, Ellabeth, let's go."

At that moment, Krystal appeared. "I'm coming, too," she said.

"Krystal!" the Riders shouted as they crowded around. "How do you feel?"

"Good as new," Krystal said. "But can someone please explain what's happening?"

While they ran to their unicorns, Willow explained everything. Then they set out after Marlow. They searched the forest, using Fayza's light magic to help them see.

Willow's eyes caught something glinting in the light. "What's that?" she said. Dismounting for a closer look, she bent down to pick up a silver drink flask. "It's engraved with the initials F.F."

Quinn pointed to the ground. "Look, footprints," she said.

"This helps prove Felina cheated in the cross-country race," Willow said. "She must have snuck out of the race and hid here until Marlow and I passed. Then she simply rejoined the race."

"Forgetting to take her flask with her," Quinn said.

"Cheaters always get found out," Ellabeth said.

"What happened at the lake, Krystal?" Willow asked. "Do you remember being bitten?"

"No," Krystal said. "I remember eating Felina's corn cakes and then going for a swim. I started getting stomach cramps. Then I went under."

"Did anyone else eat the corn cakes?" Willow asked.

"No," Quinn said. "We weren't hungry."

Willow frowned. "Why didn't you mention this before?"

"We didn't think it was important," Ellabeth said. "We thought a water snake bit Krystal. Like Felina said."

"I think Felina put something in the corn cakes to make you sick," Willow said. "And she gave you another dose in Marlow's herbal drink to keep you out of action. You just needed time to recover."

"If she cheated in the race and made Krystal sick," Quinn said, "it's possible she damaged the equipment, too."

"Or maybe Marlow and Felina are working together to confuse us," Willow said.

"What do we do now?" Ellabeth asked.

"First, we find Marlow and question him," Willow said. "Then we deal with Felina. Quinn, can Ula sense where Marlow is?"

Quinn sent Ula a mind-message.

Ula's magic whirled.

Quinn's face went pale.

"What is it?" Willow asked.

"A bear," Quinn said, "heading this way."

The sound of branches snapping made the Riders turn. A bear crashed through the trees, growling and swiping at everything in its way.

"Go!" Willow shouted.

Quinn, Krystal, and Ellabeth, who were still mounted, galloped away. Willow hobbled toward Obecky, but her sore foot gave way and she tripped, striking her head on a rock.

Dazed and in pain, Willow lay on the ground as the bear stood over her and lifted its huge paw to strike.

Willow closed her eyes.

"Aaggghhh!" A shout filled the air. Willow's eyes sprang open. She saw Marlow leap between her and the bear. "Get back! Back, I say!" he shouted.

Willow staggered to her feet. "Marlow! What are you doing?" she asked.

"Saving you," Marlow said. His eyes never left the bear. "You were about to be attacked."

"No," Willow said. "You're about to be attacked. Duck!"

Marlow ducked, barely avoiding being sliced open by the bear's claws. It roared with frustration.

Suddenly, Krystal galloped back into the clearing. Pearly-white magic whirled from Estrella's horn as she reared up and danced in circles. Mesmerized, the bear stared dumbly at the enchanting unicorn.

"Ula!" Quinn yelled as she returned with Ellabeth. "Mind-message the bear to leave."

Ula's magic whirled as she followed Quinn's request.

Grumbling and shaking its head, the bear gave a final, muted growl before dropping down on all fours and lumbering away.

Relief swept through the girls.

"Yay!" Ellabeth cheered. "We did it."

"You, um, didn't need me, did you?" Marlow asked sheepishly.

"No," Willow said. "But you were brave. Thanks."

Marlow grinned. "Next time I won't meddle in Unicorn Rider business," he said.

"Good idea," Willow said. "We've been looking for you. Did you destroy the equipment?"

"No," Marlow replied. "Felina did. I'm sure of it. I caught her cutting back into camp a short while ago. She'd been out somewhere, up to no good. When I confronted her she said something about payback for wrongs done to her family."

"We figured out she cheated in the race," said Willow. "And made Krystal sick. But we don't know why."

"You'll have to figure it out later," Marlow said. "Right now, you have to warn Queen Heart. When I caught Felina sneaking back into camp, she boasted that she planted a trap in the roadway to stop the Queen. Then she took off, yelling that I'd wrecked the tournament. I think she wants me out of the way so she has a chance of winning the cross-country race."

"Is that why you ran away?" Quinn asked.

Marlow nodded, "I panicked," he said. "And I thought I could reach Queen Heart in time to help her. Better that than being arrested."

"You really should stop trying to be a hero," Ellabeth said.

"I know," Marlow said, rolling his eyes. "From now on, I'll leave the heroics to you Riders."

"Excellent," Willow said. "Now, show us where this trap is."

• CHAPTER 11 •

THE RIDERS HURRIED THROUGH the forest on their unicorns, following Marlow.

He really is fast, Willow thought. *How did I ever hope to beat him?*

They emerged from the trees near The Fire Line volcanoes as the sun was rising.

"Felina said she set the trap near one of those volcanoes," Marlow panted.

"Look," Krystal said, pointing to the road ahead.

In the distance, the Riders spied a cloud of dust. It was the Queen's carriage, speeding toward them.

"Stay here," Willow told Marlow. "It's time for more Unicorn Rider heroics."

Using Fayza's magic to make them faster, the Riders sped toward the volcanoes.

"Ula can see the trap," Quinn shouted above the unicorn's thundering hooves. "She's sending me a mind picture."

"Which volcano, Quinn?" Willow asked.

"I can't see . . . Wait. There!" Quinn said, pointing to the middle volcano. The road curved around it and dropped sharply away into the valley below. "There's a pile of rocks across the road, behind the bend. It looks like the result of a mini avalanche, but they've been put there intentionally."

"The Queen's carriage is coming too fast," Ellabeth cried. "We won't reach it in time to stop her."

Willow's mind raced. "Maybe we can combine the unicorns' magic to blast the rocks. It will be close, but it's our only hope," she said.

"Let's do it," Ellabeth said, and the others agreed.

"Right," Willow said. "We ride as one! Now, get that unicorn magic going."

Still galloping along, the unicorns whirled magic from their horns. In a rainbow of color, magic shot into the sky, twisting like a mini tornado.

Quinn instructed Ula to use her powers to direct the magic at the rocks. Ula struggled to manage the unwieldy rainbow. It wavered and swayed, striking a row of poplar trees. The trees shattered into pieces with a bang.

Willow saw Ula double her efforts. The magic swung toward the rock pile. The unicorn strained to hold it there.

Queen Heart's carriage still rumbled down the road. Blinded by the morning sun, the driver didn't see the Riders or their magic. Willow shouted for the driver to stop, but he was too far away to hear.

On Ula's second attempt, the unicorn magic struck the rocks, blasting them to dust in a flash of brilliant light. The noise and light frightened the Queen's horses, causing them to squeal and panic. They swerved, dragging the carriage sideways across the road and throwing off the driver and footman. The shafts snapped. Still harnessed together, the four horses bolted past the Riders.

"After them, Krystal," Willow said.

Krystal wheeled Estrella around and shot after the terrified horses.

Up ahead, the horseless carriage toppled over the road edge.

"Queen Heart!" Willow gasped.

Krystal and Estrella overtook the bolting horses. Estrella's magic shimmered, enveloping the panicked horses and dazzling them with her beauty. The horses slowed and then stopped. Their sides were heaving and their nostrils flared.

Krystal collected the closest horse's bridle. She led the foursome back up the road. The driver and footman stumbled over to take them.

Willow leaped off Obecky. She peered over the embankment. The carriage was lying on its side in the long grass below, its wheels spinning uselessly.

Luggage and pieces of broken carriage were strewn everywhere. She heard groaning.

"We have to save Queen Heart," Willow said. "I'll go down and get her."

"The carriage is hanging over the ledge," Ellabeth pointed out. "Your weight will topple it."

"What about me?" Quinn said. "I'm light."

Willow frowned. She wanted to be the one to rescue Queen Heart. Just like she wanted to win the cross-country race.

But Ellabeth was right. It was too dangerous for Willow to go. Her weight might send the carriage plummeting into the valley below.

Willow searched inside herself and saw the truth.

Sometimes, no matter how hard I want to win, I can't, she thought. *Sometimes, I'm not the best person for the job. As Head Rider, I have to step back and let others shine. This is Quinn's moment. Not mine.*

"You're right," Willow said. "You go. I'll stay here and pull you up."

"Ula's telling me to hurry," Quinn said. "The carriage is about to go over the edge."

"Obecky, hold the carriage steady with your magic," Willow said.

Ellabeth tied her lasso around a tree and then around Quinn's waist. Quinn scaled down the cliff. She crawled across the overturned carriage and opened the door.

"Queen Heart, can you hear me?" Quinn glanced up at the others. "She's not moving."

Quinn climbed into the carriage. It teetered dangerously.

"Careful," Willow said. "Slow, easy movements."

Inside the carriage, Queen Heart was coming around. Her maid was lying beside her. Quinn looped the lasso around the Queen's waist and eased her through the door.

"Tie the lasso around her," Quinn called.

Together, the Riders hauled the Queen to safety. They did the same with the maid and then Quinn.

Once everyone was safe, Obecky released her hold on the carriage. It slid over the edge of the cliff and crashed into the valley below.

Willow let out a long breath. "That was close," she said. "Are you all right, Your Majesty?"

"I'm fine," Queen Heart replied. Her chin trembled. "Just shaken."

Willow explained to Queen Heart all that had been happening.

"Poor Felina," Queen Heart said. "Why would she go to such extremes?"

"Aren't you angry, Your Majesty?" Ellabeth asked. "She endangered a lot of lives."

"Thanks to you Riders, she didn't succeed," Queen Heart said gravely. "I suspect her actions are a cry for help, but I'll need to hear her story before making a final judgement."

"I wonder what she'll have to say for herself," Quinn said.

"Whatever it is, it'd better be good," Willow said.

• CHAPTER 12 •

THEY BORROWED A CARRIAGE for the Queen and her assistants from a nearby farmhouse, picking Marlow up on the way and escorting everyone to the tournament.

The moment they returned, the Riders sought Felina out. They found her practicing her archery.

"Felina," Willow said. "Queen Heart wishes to speak with you."

The Head Rider escorted Felina to Queen Heart's tent.

"We have reason to believe you've been causing trouble at this tournament," Queen Heart said to Felina. "Is this correct?"

"Your Majesty, I can explain," Felina said, her hands trembling. "I was desperate for your attention."

Queen Heart fixed the girl with a steady gaze. "So you sabotaged the tournament?" she asked.

"Yes," Felina whispered. "I'm so sorry. I didn't mean for anyone to get hurt. I only wanted to keep the Unicorn Riders occupied with other things, so I could win. I needed to speak to you. I'm worried about my brother and our farm. Please, Your Majesty." She dropped to her knees. "No one will help us."

"Why are you worried about your brother?" Queen Heart asked.

"He was injured while training for this year's tournament," Felina explained. "Our sponsor, Sir Drexitt, pushed him too hard in the joust. My brother broke both legs, several ribs, and his right arm. Sir Drexitt said he couldn't afford proper medical care. My parents are old and can't work the farm any more. My brother is the only one capable. With him injured, everything has fallen apart."

She twisted her fingers together. "Now Sir Drexitt is kicking us off our farm because we can't pay his rent," Felina continued. "I've sent him letters, pleading for mercy. I've sent you letters, Queen Heart, but they all went unanswered." Tears streamed down Felina's face. "I tried everything. I thought this would be the one sure way you would notice me and listen to me. I never meant to hurt anyone. Things just got out of control. I only meant to make Krystal ill, not to endanger her life. And I didn't mean to hurt you. I just wanted to stop the carriage to talk to you in person. When it crashed, I got scared and ran back here to camp. Please believe me."

"You sure got noticed," Ellabeth muttered, "In the wrong way."

Willow nudged her sharply to silence her.

"I never received your letters," Queen Heart said. "If I had, I would have given you proper assistance. I did receive an anonymous letter this week threatening trouble at the tournament, however. Was that from you?"

Felina nodded. "I had no way of knowing whether you received my other letters," Felina said. "I was angry that you hadn't responded, but at the same time I suspected Sir Drexitt was stopping my letters. I couldn't be sure. So I sent that threatening note anonymously in the hope that it would make it through. It also served another purpose. If you were ignoring my letters, threatening to ruin the games might finally make you take notice. Your Majesty, please understand. My brother is crippled. My parents are devastated. And Sir Drexitt has been heartless in his dealings with us. I needed to get your attention. Someway. Somehow."

"Your desperation is quite clear," Queen Heart said. "If what you say is true, Sir Drexitt has been very remiss in his duties as your brother's sponsor. And cruel in his dealings with your family. I will make sure he is punished for the way he's treated you, Felina."

"Thank you, Your Majesty," Felina said.

"And now that I'm aware of your family's situation, I will see that it is addressed," the Queen said.

"Thank you, Queen Heart, thank you," said Felina.

"You have, however, gone about this all wrong," said Queen Heart. "We will discuss your punishment and how you might make amends."

"Yes, of course," Felina agreed. "What I did was wrong. I hope you can forgive me."

"We understand you were upset," Willow said. "But instead of endangering people and cheating to get attention, you should have come to us and asked for help. You can talk to us, you know."

Fresh tears shone in Felina's eyes. "I know that now. Thank you," she said.

"You may go now, Felina," Queen Heart said. "I will call for you again later."

"Yes, Your Majesty," said Felina. With a clumsy curtsey, Felina scurried away.

"Queen Heart, there's something else I'd like to ask you to consider," Willow said. She glanced outside to where Marlow was helping contestants prepare for their events. "Marlow Grimm showed great bravery assisting us."

"Even when we didn't need it," Ellabeth piped up.

Willow smiled. "We managed perfectly fine, but Marlow was still brave and useful," said Willow. "Would you consider offering him a place in your service? He would make an excellent soldier."

The Queen raised an eyebrow.

Willow hurried on. "I know he looks unusual with those scars, but he's kind and strong," Willow said. "He has had a hard life. Valerian murdered his family."

"We didn't know!" the other Riders exclaimed.

"I value your opinion, Willow." Queen Heart inclined her head. "I shall meet with him afterward to discuss his future."

Willow grinned, confident she'd done the right thing by Marlow. "Thank you, Your Majesty," she said.

Later that day, Willow gazed out at the crowd before her. Queen Heart stood on her left, and Quinn, Krystal, and Ellabeth were on her right.

Willow admired the gold medallions she held. Each bore the image of the dancing unicorn.

It's a shame they're not for me, she thought. *But I don't need medals. I'm respected as a Unicorn Rider and Queen Heart values me. That's victory enough.*

"I'm never going to hear the end of this," Krystal whispered.

Willow laughed. "You and me both," she said.

"Can you believe it?" Quinn said. "None of us win a medal, but Ellabeth wins two."

The three friends laughed.

"You're up," Krystal said, elbowing Willow.

"Now," Willow announced, "to accept her awards for first place in hand-to-hand combat and in fencing, please congratulate Ellabeth Crisp, Unicorn Rider!"

Ellabeth eagerly accepted her medals. She held them high while the crowd cheered. Her parents stood in the front row, beaming proudly.

Next came Marlow. He'd won the cross-country, the sprint, the hurling, and the pell. Four medals.

Willow hadn't competed in the end. Her foot had become so swollen she could barely hobble around. Thanks to Obecky's magic, she was finally on the road to recovery.

After the ceremony, the crowd moved to the picnic tables set up for the end-of-tournament banquet.

Jala had arrived at the last minute, claiming she'd been too excited to stay away. As Willow stepped off the stage, her leader called her over. "Have you enjoyed the tournament?" Jala asked.

Willow shrugged. "I could have done without Felina's antics," Willow said.

"I bet," Jala replied. "But in the end, you used quick thinking and saved the Queen. That's the important thing."

"Part of me still wishes I'd won a medal," Willow said.

"Life isn't about glory, it's about good deeds," said Jala. "Besides, you won something far more important than a medal."

"Which is?" Willow asked.

Jala pointed. "A friend," she said.

"Sorry to interrupt, Honorable Rider," Marlow said as he walked over.

"I'll leave you to it," Jala said as she strode off.

"What's with the 'Honorable Rider' stuff?" Willow asked.

"Thanks to you, I'm a trainee in the Queen's army now," Marlow replied. "I'm simply showing my respect."

Willow touched the medals dangling around his neck. "It was your courage and skill that got you noticed. Not me," she said. She paused for a moment before continuing. "I'm sorry it took me so long to see the real you."

Marlow blushed. "Does that make us friends now?" he asked.

"Of course." Willow laughed. "Always." And they shook hands to seal their pact.

Glossary

anonymous (uh-NON-uh-muhss)—written, done, or given by a person whose name is not known or made public

arrogant (AR-uh-guhnt)—exaggerating one's own self worth or importance, often in an overbearing manner

concoction (kahn-KAHKT-shuhn)—something made by combining several ingredients

confidential (kahn-fi-DEN-shuhl)—secret

hoax (HOHKS)—a trick to make people believe something that is not true

joust (JOUST)—a contest between two knights riding horses and armed with lances

rival (RYE-vuh)—a person who is trying to achieve the same goal or trying to be better than someone else; a competitor

sabotage (SAB-uh-tahzh)—damage or destruction of property that is done on purpose

sarcasm (SAHR-kaz-uhm)—humor that points out someone's mistakes or weaknesses

stamina (STAM-uh-nuh)—the energy and strength to keep doing something for a long time

UNICORN RIDERS

UNICORN RIDERS
Ellabeth's Test
Aleesah Darlison

UNICORN RIDERS
Krystal's Choice
Aleesah Darlison

UNICORN RIDERS
Quinn's Riddles
Aleesah Darlison

UNICORN RIDERS
Willow's Challenge
Aleesah Darlison

UNICORN RIDERS
Quinn's Truth
Aleesah Darlison

UNICORN RIDERS
Willow's Victory
Aleesah Darlison

UNICORN RIDERS
Ellabeth's Light
Aleesah Darlison

UNICORN RIDERS
Krystal's Charge
Aleesah Darlison

COLLECT THE SERIES!

~~ussi~~ion Questions

~~...~~ Willow learn about herself as the Head
~~...~~ in the story?

~~...~~ w did Willow figure out that Felina was the
~~...~~boteur?

~~...~~. In what ways did Marlow overcome challenges from
his past and become successful?

Writing Prompts

1. If you were a Unicorn Rider, would you want to be
the Head Rider? Why or why not?

2. Willow learned that Marlow was a good person after
she got to know him. Have you ever changed your
opinion about someone after getting to know them?

3. If you were competing in the Spring Tournament,
which event would you participate in?